This book belongs to
my friend:

_____

Emotions

Published by Scholastic Inc., 90 Old Sherman Turnpike, Danbury, CT 06816

scholastic and associated logos are trademarks and/or registered trademarks of Scholastic Inc.

ISBN 0-7172-9869-8

Printed in the U.S.A.

First Scholastic Printing, June 2006

The Big Pony Race

by
Erica David

illustrated by
Jason Fruchter

SCHOLASTIC INC.

New York Toronto London Auckland Sydney
Mexico City New Delhi Hong Kong Buenos Aires

One day, as Dora and Boots were playing in Dora's backyard, they noticed a trail of hoof prints. "I wonder who these belong to," said Dora. They followed the trail to find a little pony standing under a tree.

"*Hola*, I'm Penny," the pony said. "I was on my way to Pony Field for the Big Pony Race, but I got lost."
"Don't worry, we'll help you," Dora replied.

"Who do we call when we don't know which way to go?" Dora asked.

"Map!" Boots shouted.

At the sound of his name, Map popped out of Backpack's pocket.

"I can tell you how to get to Pony Field," Map said.
"First, you need to pass the Prickly Hedge. Then, cross
the Mud Pit, and that's how you get to Pony Field."
"*¡Gracias!*" Dora exclaimed.

Dora, Boots, and Penny began walking along a path. Before long, the Prickly Hedge stopped them in their tracks.

"How are we going to get past the Prickly Hedge?" Dora asked.

"I know," Penny said. "I'll carry you on my back and jump over it."

Dora and Boots climbed onto Penny's back. Penny started to gallop toward the Prickly Hedge, but just before she reached it, she came to a sudden stop.

"What's wrong?" Dora asked.

"The hedge is really high," Penny said. "I'm not sure I can jump over."

"I know you can do it," Dora said. "We'll help you. When it's time to jump, we'll shout '¡*Salta!*'"

Penny took a deep breath and ran toward the hedge again.

"¡*Salta!*" Dora and Boots shouted.

This time, Penny
jumped right over the hedge.
     "You did it!" Dora and
Boots cheered.

Dora, Boots, and Penny soon spotted the Mud Pit.
"The Mud Pit is too wide to walk around," Dora said.
"How will we get across?" Boots asked.
"I know," Penny replied. "I'll trot across the logs."

"These logs look kind of slippery," Penny said nervously.

"We'll count the logs together as you walk
across so you won't be worried," said Dora.

"*Uno* . . . *dos* . . . *tres* . . . *cuatro* . . . *cinco!*" Dora and
Boots counted as Penny crossed the Mud Pit.
"*Muy bien*, Penny!" Dora cheered. "We made it across!"

Dora, Boots, and Penny arrived at Pony Field just
in time for the race. Penny hurried to take her place
at the starting line along with the other ponies.

"The first pony to reach the other side of the field wins!" called the announcer. "On your mark, get set, go!"

The ponies took off
running across the field. Within
seconds, they came to a series of gates.
    "Those gates are high," Penny thought to herself.

Then she heard Dora and Boots cheering for her.
"*¡Salta!*" they shouted.
Penny took a deep breath and leaped
over the gates.

Next, Penny raced
around a bend. In front of
her was a large pool of water. The other
horses ran around the pool, but Penny knew that it
was quicker to cross the planks.

"How do I trot across all these planks without tripping?"
she wondered.

"Count them out, Penny!" called Dora and Boots.
"*Uno . . . dos . . . tres . . . cuatro . . . cinco!*" Penny
counted as she trotted across the planks.

Penny galloped into the home stretch. She could see the finish line just ahead. She ran as fast as she could to pass the pony beside her.

"Go Penny!" Dora and Boots cheered as she took the lead.

Penny crossed the finish line in first place.
Dora and Boots ran to congratulate her.
"You did it!" Boots exclaimed.

"No, *we* did it." Penny replied. "Thanks for your help. We make a great team!"

"Hooray!" Dora cheered. *"Lo hicimos!* We did it!"

1st Place

Nick Jr. Play-to-Learn™ Fundamentals

Skills every child needs, in stories every child will love!

colors + shapes
Recognizing and identifying basic shapes and colors in the context of a story.

emotions
Learning to identify and understand a wide range of emotions: happy, sad, excited, frustrated, etc.

imagination
Fostering creative thinking skills through role-play and make-believe.

123 math
Recognizing early math in the world around us: patterns, shapes, numbers, sequences.

music + movement
Celebrating the sounds and rhythms of music and dance.

physical
Building coordination and confidence through physical activity and play.

problem solving
Using critical thinking skills (observing, listening, following directions) to make predictions and solve problems.

reading + language
Developing a lifelong love of reading through high interest stories and characters.

science
Fostering curiosity and an interest in the natural world around us.

social skills + cultural diversity
Developing respect for others as unique, interesting people.

Emotions

Conversation Spark

Questions and activities for play–to–learn parenting.

Dora and Boots were so happy when they got to Pony Field with Penny in time for the big race! Do you remember another time in the story when Dora and Boots felt happy? Can you find a happy face in the story?

For more parent and kid-friendly activities, go to www.nickjr.com.

ENGLISH/SPANISH GLOSSARY and PRONUNCIATION GUIDE

ENGLISH	SPANISH	PRONUNCIATION
Hello	Hola	OH-lah
Thank you	Gracias	GRAH-see-ahs
Jump	Salta	SAHL-tah
One	Uno	OO-noh
Two	Dos	DOHS
Three	Tres	TRES
Four	Quatro	KWAH-troh
Five	Cinco	SEEN-koh
Very well	Muy Bien	MOO-ee BEE-ayn
We did it	Lo hicimos	LO-ee SEE-mohs
Good-bye	Adiós	Ah-dee-OHS